Sensitive Sam

Written & illustrated by

Marla Roth-Fisch

FUTURE HORIZONS INC.

Sensitive Sam

All marketing and publishing rights guaranteed to and reserved by

FUTURE HORIZONS INC.

721 W. Abram Street
Arlington, Texas 76013
800-489-0727
817-277-0727
817-277-2270 (fax)
E-mail: info@FHautism.com
www.FHautism.com

ISBN: 978-1-932565-86-7

A Note for
Parents and Educators

Sensitive Sam is written from the perspective of a young boy with Sensory Processing Disorder (SPD) and his daily challenges. It is designed to be a book that adults can read to children, and children can then read and review on their own.

The happy ending will inspire hope for your family and promote ongoing discussion about sensory issues.

Enjoy!

Hi, they call me Sensitive Sam!
I'm always sad or mad.
A lot of things do bother me
But I don't mean to be bad!

The littlest things are tough for me
All day and all night.
No matter what I say or do,
Things just don't FEEL right.

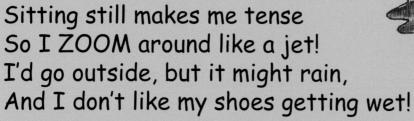

Sitting still makes me tense
So I ZOOM around like a jet!
I'd go outside, but it might rain,
And I don't like my shoes getting wet!

Oh no! The drapes are open
And the sun is just too bright!
Oh no! My jeans are SCRATCHING me
And they're way too tight!

Oh no! I can't wear this red shirt!
There's a sharp tag on the inside.

Oh no! I'm cold! I need my SOFT scarf
Before I can go outside.

Oh no! Please don't use that comb.
It pulls and hurts my head!
It's okay to brush it, though.
Please use this instead.

Oh no! Those eggs smell really bad!
My stomach hurts when I get close.
And they're too squishy and mushy to eat.
I can't eat those! They're gross!

Oh no! While in the bathroom
It can get too noisy to hear.
The loud sound of the toilet FLUSH
Can really hurt my ears.

And that is just my morning,
Getting ready for the day.
My mom and dad look upset.
They say, "This is not okay!"

The school day is no better.
One day, my class played with clay.
"Oh no! That's too messy!" I said.
"No, I don't want to play!"

At recess I was sad because
My boots felt way too tight.
So I grabbed and pulled, and grabbed and pulled,
And pulled with all my might!

Oh no! My boot went flying off
And then my boot was wet!
I turned all red and wanted to cry.
I hate feeling upset.

I came in after recess
With one boot off, one boot on.
My teacher could not understand
Why I left one on the lawn.

Oh no! She called my parents!
But they were more concerned than mad.
They talked about ways to help me.
They didn't yell at me for being bad.

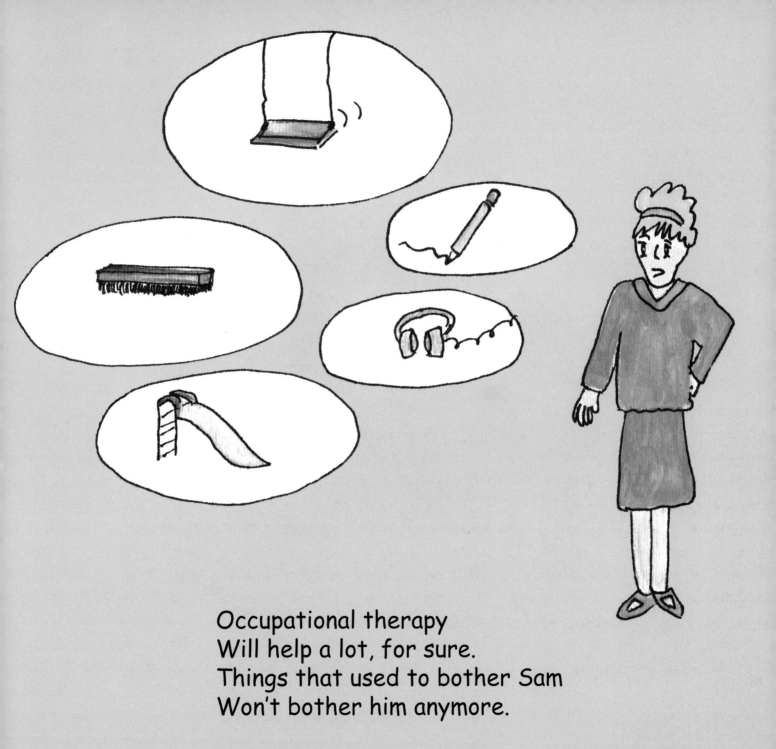

Occupational therapy
Will help a lot, for sure.
Things that used to bother Sam
Won't bother him anymore.

I told my dad that I was scared
And asked, "Will I be okay?"
He said, "Of course! In fact, you will feel
A little bit better each day!"

So my parents made an appointment
With a therapist called an "OT."
When we went for the first time,
There were kids there just like me!

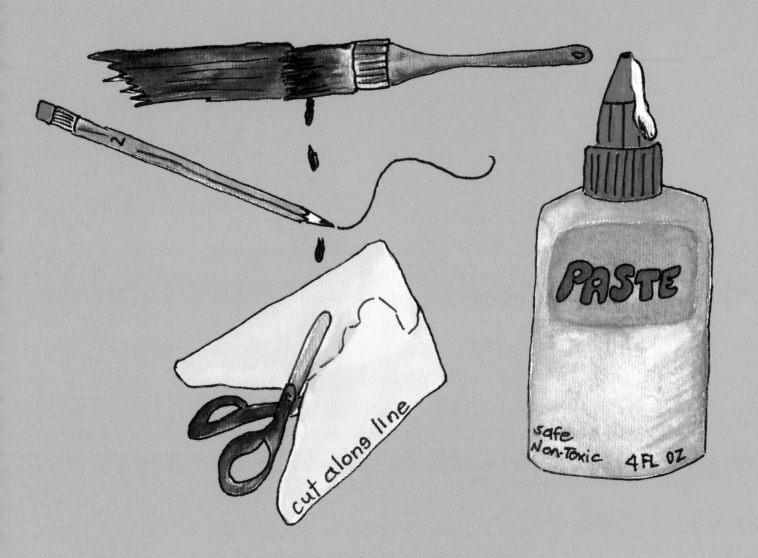

I cut-and-pasted, I painted, I drew,
I even ran around!
The OT watched the way I played
And wrote a lot of things down.

Sensory Diet Activity program

1. Brush arms, hands, legs, feet, and back with firm touch
2. Have Mom or Dad pull and push on arms, and legs
3. Swim and splash, dunk head
4. Finger paint with pudding
5. Enjoy swings, see-saw, and slide
6. Jump on trampoline
7. Listen to music and dance
8. Smell different spices and scents
9. Look people in the eyes when you talk
10. Taste a couple of new foods

HAVE FUN!
See you at your next appointment.

She talked to my parents and talked to me,
And gave us a list of activities.
The list was called a "Sensory Diet."
It would help me with my sensitivities!

We did the things on the Sensory Diet
Some different, and some new.
It took some work but I FEEL better!
My OT said, "Good for you!"

My parents are so proud of me
As the weeks go by.
They believe in me and see
A "special twinkle" in my eye!

Now mornings aren't so terrible.
Mom says I'm doing great!
I take my time, get ready,
And eat my breakfast from my plate.

Treating sensory challenges
Takes some patience, and love, too.
And now I LIKE doing lots of things
I used to hate to do!

Take it from me, Sensitive Sam,
That things will be okay.

By doing things a little differently,
I can have fun EVERY day!

Helpful Information for Parents and Educators

Glossary

Occupational Therapy – Using meaningful activities to help people with disabilities integrate all their senses to achieve the highest possible function.

Occupational Therapist (OT) - A registered health professional who evaluates, diagnoses, and develops treatment plans for patients in need of therapy.

Sensory Processing Disorder (SPD) – A neurological disorder that results from the brain's inability to interpret information received from the seven basic sensory systems. These sensory systems are accountable for detecting sights, smells, sounds, temperatures, tastes, position, movements of the body, and pain. The brain then forms a blended picture of this information so that the body makes sense of its surroundings and responds to them appropriately. The continuous relationship between behavior and brain functioning is called sensory integration (SI), a theory that was first pioneered by A. Jean Ayres, Ph.D., OTR in the 1960s.

Sensory Diet – A sensory diet is an activity plan designed especially for a child with Sensory Processing Disorder. The diet offers the best combination of sensations at the appropriate level of intensity for the child. In order to provide input to the brain to stimulate growth, sensory diets may include: firm brushing using a soft brush, joint compression, spinning, swinging, oral stimulation, playing in sand and beans (both wet and dry), deep pressure massage and touch, jumping, music therapy, rolling in ball pits, water play, and various other enjoyable and educational activities.

Sensory Processing Disorder Website Resources

www.FHsensory.com
www.out-of-sync-child.com
www.sensorycomfort.com
www.ateachabout.com
www.southpawenterprises.com
www.zerotothree.org

www.spdfoundation.net
www.aota.org
www.alertprogram.com
www.otawatertown.com
www.devdelay.org
www.therapyshoppe.com